D0578638

ILL DEC 02

GAYLORD MG

Snipp, Snapp, Snurr
and the
GINGERBREAD

MAJ LINDMAN

ALBERT WHITMAN & COMPANY
Morton Grove, Illinois

The Snipp, Snapp, Snurr Books
Snipp, Snapp, Snurr and the Red Shoes
Snipp, Snapp, Snurr and the Gingerbread
Snipp, Snapp, Snurr and the Buttered Bread (March 1995)
Snipp, Snapp, Snurr Learn to Swim (March 1995)

The Flicka, Ricka, Dicka Books
Flicka, Ricka, Dicka and the New Dotted Dresses
Flicka, Ricka, Dicka and the Three Kittens
Flicka, Ricka, Dicka Bake a Cake (March 1995)
Flicka, Ricka, Dicka and the Little Dog (March 1995)

ISBN 0-8075-7493-7
LC 94-13627

The text is set in 23′ Futura Book
and 12′ Bookman Light Italic.

A Snipp, Snapp, Snurr Book

She handed them a coin.

Snipp, Snapp, and Snurr were three little boys who lived in Sweden. Their hair was yellow. Their cheeks were pink. Their eyes were blue.

One morning they put on their red shirts and blue trousers and red socks to take a walk. Soon they met their next–door neighbor.

"Good morning, Snipp, Snapp, and Snurr," she said kindly. "Where are you going this nice morning?"

"Good morning to you," said the three little boys. "We haven't yet decided where we're going."

"I see," she said. "Well, here's an idea. Take this coin, go to the baker, and buy whatever you want most."

She handed them a coin and went slowly on down the street.

Well," said Snipp, Snapp, and Snurr together. "Let's all go to the bakery!"

Off they ran, straight to the village baker.

"Good morning, Mr. Baker," they said as they walked in.

"We have come for cookies," said Snipp.

"We would like pie," said Snapp.

"No—gingerbread," said Snurr.

"Gingerbread is fine," said the baker. "I am making it now. Come out to the kitchen and watch me stir it before I put it into the oven."

Snipp, Snapp, and Snurr followed the baker to the kitchen. They all climbed up on one chair so they could watch him more carefully.

They all climbed up on one chair.

Perhaps Snipp was too far back on the chair to see well, and so he tried to lean forward. Maybe Snapp and Snurr were crowding each other to get a better view of the dark brown batter. Perhaps the chair slipped on the shiny kitchen floor.

Snipp, Snapp, and Snurr never could tell quite how it happened.

But in a moment the chair was tipping forward, and the three little boys felt themselves falling—falling headfirst into the dark brown gingerbread batter!

The baker was so surprised that he threw up his hands. His white cap flew off his head.

His white cap flew off his head.

He fell on the floor in amazement. As he sat there, Snipp, Snapp, and Snurr climbed out of the mixing trough. They were not hurt.

But they were covered from head to toe with gingerbread batter. Their red shirts and blue trousers and red socks were all dark brown. Their faces, arms, and legs were the same dark brown color.

"Let's go home," said Snipp, "before the baker can scold us."

"Let's run," said Snapp.

"Hurry!" said Snurr.

Across the shiny floor they ran, out into the street.

"Let's go home," said Snipp, "before the baker can scold us."

Snipp, Snapp, and Snurr, all covered with dark brown batter, ran across town. They looked just like gingerbread boys who had come to life.

An old woman sat at the corner selling apples. She could not believe her eyes when she saw the three gingerbread boys. She was so frightened that she dropped her two baskets, and the apples rolled down the street.

A black cat saw the three little boys and ran away as fast as he could.

The policeman took one look at the gingerbread boys and hurried off, too. Even he did not know what to do about three gingerbread boys on the streets of his town!

The apples rolled down the street.

A big black-and-white dog hurried toward them. He smelled the rich brown gingerbread.

Now that big black-and-white dog was very fond of gingerbread. So he ran after Snipp, Snapp, and Snurr.

Poor Snipp, Snapp, and Snurr! How frightened they were to find a big dog chasing them!

Down the street they ran, faster and faster. The dog ran faster and faster, too.

Snurr, who was a little behind the others, stumbled and fell.

Just as the big dog came very near, a golden coach drawn by four white horses drove by. A beautiful Princess was in the coach.

A beautiful Princess was in the coach.

The coach drew up beside Snipp, Snapp, and Snurr. Two footmen helped them get in.

With a crack of the whip, they were off—straight to the palace! The Princess was delighted with the three little boys. "I have always wanted to see a gingerbread boy," she said. "And now I have three live gingerbread boys here with me! It is the nicest thing that could happen! We must have a party."

Soon Snipp, Snapp, and Snurr were drinking hot chocolate and eating fruit and cakes in the royal dining room.

The Princess sat at the head of the table. She wore a pink dress and her golden crown, and she told them fairy tales.

The Princess sat at the head of the table.

When Snipp, Snapp, and Snurr had heard all her stories, the Princess helped them back into the golden coach. She called her two footmen and told them to take the three little gingerbread boys home.

So for the second time that day, Snipp, Snapp, and Snurr rode through town in a golden coach.

They looked out of the window as they rode along.

They saw the old woman with her apples.

The town policeman saluted them.

The black–and–white dog who liked gingerbread sat with his ears pricked up and watched them.

They looked out of the window as they rode along.

When the golden coach reached home, the footmen helped the gingerbread boys get out. After they were inside the house, the four white horses pranced back to the palace, their silver bells tinkling.

Almost before Snipp, Snapp, and Snurr had a chance to tell Mother about their wonderful party, they found themselves in the big bathtub.

Mother used soap, plenty of hot water, and a big scrub brush. Soon the gingerbread boys vanished. In their place were the three little boys who had gone for a walk that morning.

Their hair was yellow. Their cheeks were pink. Their eyes were blue. And they were smiling happily because the brown gingerbread boys were gone forever.

Mother used soap, plenty of hot water, and a big scrub brush.

Soon Mother tucked each little boy into bed. And as he lay there warm and clean and sleepy, Snipp said softly, "I am glad—" Before he could finish, he had gone to sleep.

Snapp murmured sleepily, "I am glad I am not—" and his eyelids closed in the middle of the sentence.

So Snurr finished, "I am glad I am not a gingerbread boy." Then he, too, was asleep.

As the three little boys slept, the baker with his white cap and big spoon, the policeman with his long sword, the Princess in a pink dress and golden crown, the old woman and her apples, gingerbread men, gingerbread ladies, and gingerbread cats all danced through their dreams!

...all danced through their dreams!